Lisa the Lollipop Fairy

Special thanks to Narinder Dhami

No part of this publication may be reproduced, stored in a retrieval
system, or transmitted in any form or by any means, electronic,
mechanical, photocopying, recording, or otherwise, without written
permission of the publisher. For information regarding permission,
write to Rainbow Magic Limited, c/o HIT Entertainment, 830
South Greenville Avenue, Allen, TX 75002-3320.

ISBN 978-0-545-60531-1

12 11 10 9 8 7 6 5 4 3 2 1   14 15 16 17 18 19/0

Printed in China   68

This edition first printing, March 2014

Lisa
the Lollipop
Fairy

by Daisy Meadows

SCHOLASTIC INC.

The Fairyland Palace

Candy Land

Goblins' ice cream truck

Market booths

Charlie's ice cream truck

Kirsty's House

Wetherbury Village

I have a plan to make a mess
And cause the fairies much distress.
I'm going to take their charms away
And make my dreams come true today!

I'll build a castle made of sweets,
And ruin the fairies' silly treats.
I just don't care how much they whine,
Their cakes and candies will be mine!

Contents

Not So Sweet!

"I can't *wait* for you to meet my aunt, Rachel!" Kirsty Tate exclaimed, beaming at her best friend, Rachel Walker. Rachel had arrived that morning to spend spring break with Kirsty in the pretty village of Wetherbury. "Mom invited her to come to lunch today, so you'll be able to ask

Aunt Helen all about Candy Land."

Rachel grinned. "I can't wait to meet
Aunt Helen, either," she replied.
"Working in a candy factory must be
one of the most wonderful jobs in the
whole world!"

"I guess it's *almost* as wonderful as being
a fairy," Kirsty said, and the girls shared
a secret smile.
They'd had many
thrilling adventures
with their fairy
friends, and hoped to
have a lot more.

"The Candy Land factory is on a hill
overlooking Wetherbury," Kirsty
explained. "Aunt Helen gets lots of free
treats, and she always brings a big bagful
whenever she comes to visit."

"I'm looking forward to meeting her even more now!" Rachel laughed.

Just then, the doorbell rang and the girls rushed to answer it. Outside stood a smiling blonde woman holding a bulging pink-and-white striped shopping bag. CANDY LAND was written across the side of the bag in sparkly silver glitter.

"Hi, Kirsty," Aunt Helen said, giving her a big hug. "And you must be Rachel." She hugged Rachel, too. "I've heard so much about you from Kirsty."

"I've heard lots about you, too," Rachel replied, smiling.

"Then I'm sure Kirsty told you all

about Candy Land!" Aunt Helen said, her big blue eyes twinkling. "I thought

you might like to try some of our treats." She handed the bag to the girls. Rachel and Kirsty peeked eagerly inside. They could see lollipops, chocolate bars, and piles of other candies wrapped in shiny colored paper. But to their dismay, the treats looked crushed and crumpled, and not at all appetizing. Most unexpected of all, there was a horrible smell inside the bag that made both girls gasp! *What could that*

smell be? Rachel wondered, trying not to wrinkle her nose in disgust. The candy looked and smelled like rotting garbage! But she didn't want to complain when Aunt Helen had been  so nice to bring them the treats. Kirsty was trying to smile politely at her aunt, too.

"Maybe we should wait until after lunch to try them," Kirsty suggested, closing the bag quickly.

Aunt Helen's face fell. "The candies are

really bad, aren't they?"
She sighed. "Girls,
something's gone terribly
wrong at Candy Land.
All of the treats look,
smell, and taste
absolutely awful!"

Rachel and Kirsty were
too shocked to say anything.

"We've had lots of complaints," Aunt
Helen went on, looking more and more
upset. "Tracy Twist from the village
candy shop even called the factory to tell
us that her customers were *very*
unhappy."

"Did the factory change the candy
recipes?" Rachel asked.

Aunt Helen shook her head. "Our

candies have been made the same way for years," she replied. "All the ingredients are still exactly the same. That's why it's so strange!"

"That *is* strange," Kirsty remarked, frowning. The treats from Candy Land were usually delicious. *What is going on?* she wondered.

Mrs. Tate had prepared a delicious lunch. As they ate, Rachel and Kirsty were glad to see that Aunt Helen began to cheer up. After lunch, Aunt Helen said good-bye and hurried back to work at the candy factory. Meanwhile, the girls went up to Kirsty's bedroom, bringing the Candy Land bag with them.

"Let's look through the candies," Kirsty

said. "Maybe some of them aren't so bad." She and Rachel sat down on the rug and dumped out the bag.

Wrinkling her nose because of the awful smell, Rachel picked up a chocolate bar. She unwrapped the gold foil and took a cautious bite.

"That's gross!" Rachel spluttered, making a face. "It tastes like dishwashing liquid, really nasty and soapy."

Kirsty chose a lollipop covered in a shiny gold wrapper. The lollipop was bent out of shape and cracked across the middle, and the wrapper was ripped. The label stuck on the front said STRAWBERRY.

"Here goes nothing!" Kirsty murmured, pulling off the wrapper. She licked the lollipop, then groaned. "It smells like old socks—and it tastes like them, too!"

"Let's not try anything else," Rachel said. "The others could be even worse!"

Disappointed, the girls began scooping the candies back into the bag. The gold wrapper from the soapy chocolate bar was lying on the rug, and as Rachel went to pick it up, she thought she saw the wrapper move!

Rachel blinked and looked again. Yes, the chocolate bar wrapper was definitely moving on its own! Rachel carefully lifted the wrapper. Underneath, she saw a familiar little figure waving up at her.

"Look, Kirsty, it's Honey the Candy Fairy!" Rachel exclaimed, excited to see their old friend.

Kirsty's eyes widened in surprise. "It's great to see you, Honey!" she said. The girls had been on some wonderful adventures with Honey and the other Party Fairies. They'd helped them retrieve their magic party bags from Jack Frost's goblins.

"Hello, girls." Honey fluttered up to perch on the edge of Kirsty's bed. "I bet you can guess why I'm here, can't you?"

"Because of the horrible candy

from Candy Land?" asked Rachel.

Honey nodded. "Strange things are happening in Fairyland!"

She sighed. "We're in trouble again, girls, and we need your help. Will you come with me?"

"Of course!" Kirsty said immediately, and Rachel nodded.

"You're our very best friends in the human world!" Honey said gratefully. "Let's go right away, and I'll explain everything as soon as we get there."

With a flick of Honey's wand, a shower of fairy sparkles swept over the three friends. Rachel and Kirsty grinned at each other. They were off to Fairyland!

Candy
Castle

A few moments later, Rachel, Kirsty,
and Honey floated down into the
Fairyland Candy Factory. This was a
beautiful, magical orchard where all the
candy and yummy treats grew on trees.
The girls had been to the orchard before,
and had been amazed by all the candy
hanging in clusters among the light green
sugared leaves. But this time it looked
very different.

"What happened?" Rachel asked,
looking around the orchard in dismay.
The girls could see that the candy trees
looked wilted, their sugared leaves
withering on the branches. The candy
growing on the trees looked pale and
sickly instead of fresh and delicious.
Kirsty reached up and touched a pink-
and-white marshmallow dangling from
a branch over her head.

"The marshmallows are rock hard!"
she said, shocked.

"And the jawbreakers are as soft as butter," added Rachel, who was standing beneath a jawbreaker tree. She also noticed that all the chocolates on the tree next to her were melting into a gooey mess and dripping from the branches, leaving puddles on the ground. Even the chocolate fountain was spouting thick gray sludge instead of glossy brown chocolate. This was just like what was happening at Candy Land!

King Oberon and Queen Titania were standing next to the chocolate fountain, deep in discussion with seven other fairies. They all looked extremely worried until the queen noticed Honey, Kirsty, and Rachel hurrying toward them.

"Girls, you're here!" Queen Titania gasped with relief. "We really need your help. Our beautiful Candy Factory is ruined!"

"And the day after tomorrow is a special royal festival called Treat Day," the king explained. "We give a basket of special treats to every fairy in Fairyland as thanks for all their hard work. It will be a disaster if there is no candy for the treat baskets!"

The seven fairies nearby looked even

more anxious. Their wings drooped miserably. Honey turned to Rachel and Kirsty. "Girls, meet my special helpers, the Sugar and Spice Fairies," she announced, pointing at each fairy in turn with her wand. "Lisa the Lollipop Fairy, Esme the Ice Cream Fairy, Coco the Cupcake Fairy, Clara the Chocolate Fairy, Madeline the Cookie Fairy, Layla the Cotton Candy Fairy, and Nina the Birthday Cake Fairy."

"Welcome, girls," the fairies chorused, waving.

"We hope you can help us," Lisa the Lollipop Fairy added. She was a pretty little fairy with curly blonde hair. She wore a silky green dress with colorful pink, yellow, and purple stripes, tied in the front with a big purple bow.

"Is Jack Frost up to his nasty tricks again?" Kirsty asked, and all the fairies nodded sadly.

"He's stolen our seven magical charms!" Lisa explained. "He wants all of our delicious treats for himself, to use for a very special project."

"What special project?" Rachel asked curiously.

Honey led the girls over to one of the

pools of melted chocolate on the ground.
She waved her wand
and gradually the
brown puddle became
clear. Then an image
began to appear!
Rachel and Kirsty
could see the
Fairyland
stream surrounded
by lush green hills.

"Look!" Honey pointed at one of the
hills. "See that castle?"

Rachel and Kirsty nodded and peered
more closely. On top of the hill, a huge
castle was taking shape. It was only half
built, but there was something very
strange about it.

"The castle is made of sweet treats!"

Kirsty exclaimed suddenly. "Rachel, see the cupcake turrets and the doors made of cookies?"

Rachel nodded. "And the towers are ice-cream cones!" she added.

The girls could see Jack Frost's goblins dashing around the castle with wheelbarrows of cupcakes, ice-cream cones, chocolate bars, cotton candy, and other  goodies. Jack Frost was standing on the scaffolding, yelling at them.

"Hurry, you lazy good-for-nothings!"

he shouted. "I want my castle finished as quickly as possible. I've been planning it for ages. Sweet treats are one of my favorite things! Now bring me a lemon cupcake—I'm hungry!"

"See that necklace around Jack Frost's neck?" Honey pointed her wand at the image in the chocolate pool. Rachel and Kirsty looked closely at the necklace. It had seven glittering candy charms on it. "Those are the Sugar and Spice Fairies' magical charms!" Honey went on.

One of the goblins rushed over and handed Jack Frost a cupcake. "I bet those pesky fairies will try to get their magical charms back before Treat Day," the goblin pointed out.

Jack Frost gave a roar of rage. "Treat Day is canceled!" he snapped. "And I'll make *sure* those silly fairies and their human friends don't interfere!" With that, Jack Frost waved his wand, and a bolt of icy magic surrounded him. When the frosty air melted away, Rachel and Kirsty saw that the Sugar and Spice Fairies' magical charms had disappeared from the necklace Jack Frost was wearing.

"Now those charms are safe in the hands of my goblins!" Jack Frost cackled smugly. "They'll be hidden in the human world, so the Sugar and Spice Fairies will never see them again!"

Tracy Twist's Candy Shop

King Oberon sighed as the image in the pool of chocolate faded. "So you see, girls, Treat Day will be ruined unless our Sugar and Spice Fairies get their magical charms back," he explained. "Without them, the Fairyland Candy Factory will simply wither away."

"All yummy treats in the human world will be ruined, too," Lisa the Lollipop Fairy chimed in. "Just like the ones from Candy Land."

27

"Girls, will you help the Sugar and Spice Fairies save Treat Day?" Queen Titania asked hopefully.

The girls nodded. "We'll do our best," Kirsty replied, determined, and all the fairies clapped happily.

"Lisa will return to Wetherbury with you," Honey said, pointing her wand at Rachel and Kirsty. "Thank you, girls!" With that, a stream of magical fairy dust whisked Lisa and the girls away, the good-luck wishes of the other fairies ringing in their ears.

"Where should we start searching for

the magical charms?" Rachel wondered
aloud as soon as they were back in
Kirsty's bedroom.

Lisa thought for a moment. "What
about the village candy shop?" she
suggested. "The goblins might try to hide
my magic lollipop charm among all the
real lollipops there."

"Good idea!" Kirsty agreed. Lisa
zipped over to hide in the pocket of
Rachel's skirt,
and they hurried
downstairs. Kirsty
quickly asked her
mom for permission
to go to the candy
shop. When Mrs. Tate said yes, the three
friends headed out right away.

"We have to find all seven magical

charms," Rachel said with a frown as she and Kirsty walked down High Street. "Imagine a world where all candy always tasted horrible? It would be *awful!*"

Kirsty nudged her. "Look, Rachel," she murmured. "See those kids coming toward us? They're carrying bags from the candy shop."

The girls watched as the group of kids came closer. Two of them were unwrapping chocolate bars. The youngest of the three, a little girl, was holding an ice-cream cone.

"Ew! That tastes soapy!" one of the kids complained after taking a big bite of chocolate.

"So does mine," the other agreed. "It's the worst chocolate I've ever had in my whole life!"

The little girl took one lick of her ice-cream cone and burst into tears. "It tastes gross!" she wailed.

"Oh, no!" Lisa murmured anxiously from inside Rachel's pocket.

"This must be happening *everywhere*," Kirsty pointed out. "The sooner we get all the magical charms back to the Sugar

31

and Spice Fairies, the sooner the treats
will taste good again!"

Kirsty opened the door of the village
candy shop, and she and Rachel stepped
inside. The store was completely empty.
The owner, Tracy Twist, sat at the
counter looking glum. The store was
packed with different kinds of candy and
treats in big glass jars. Boxes of
chocolates, cupcakes, and cookies were
stacked all
around. There
were lots of
different
flavors of ice
cream to
choose from,
and even a
cotton candy

machine. But the girls couldn't see a
single lollipop.

"Hi, girls,"
said Tracy.
She looked at
Kirsty. "I bet
your aunt
Helen has told
you all about
the problems
with the Candy
Land treats?"
Kirsty nodded,
and Tracy gave a big sigh. "I'm losing all
my customers because everything tastes
so awful!" Tracy went on. "And the
worst part is, no one seems to know
why."

"Well, we've come to buy some

lollipops," Kirsty said, glancing around the store. "Do you have any, Tracy?"

Tracy shook her head. "I sold all my lollipops this morning to a group of boys," she replied. "I don't know who they were, but they must belong to some sort of club. They were all wearing matching green clothes."

Rachel and Kirsty exchanged an excited glance. Goblins?

"They started eating the lollipops before they even left the shop." Tracy frowned. "They were licking their lips and saying how wonderful they tasted! I was really surprised, because I've had so many complaints about the other candy. Maybe there were a few good ones in that batch of lollipops from Candy Land after all." She shrugged. "My mom used to run this shop. She'd be so disappointed to know that this has happened." Tracy looked around the shop sadly.

"Those goblins have my magical charm—that's why the lollipops they bought tasted so good!" Lisa whispered to the girls from Rachel's pocket. "But where are those goblins *now*?"

A Lollipop Trail

"Did the boys say where they were going, Tracy?" asked Rachel.

Tracy shook her head. "No, they didn't."

"Well, thanks, anyway," said Kirsty. "I'm sure that all the treats in your shop will be just as delicious as they used to be soon."

"I hope so!" Tracy sighed.

The girls gave her reassuring smiles and hurried outside.

"We're on the goblins' trail!" Kirsty said excitedly. "But I wonder which way they went when they came out of the candy shop?"

Both girls glanced around, but they couldn't see any flashes of green that might be goblins. Then Rachel gave a yelp.

"Did you spot a goblin?" Kirsty asked eagerly.

"No, but I *did* spot this!" Rachel replied. She bent down and picked up a lollipop stick lying on the sidewalk. "And look, there's another one up there."

"The goblins are gobbling all the lollipops and leaving a trail of lollipop sticks behind!" Lisa exclaimed, peeking out of Rachel's pocket. "We can find them by following the trail. But it'll be faster if I turn you into fairies. We can fly much quicker than we can walk!"

There was no one around to see as Lisa whirled up out of Rachel's pocket and hovered above the girls, sprinkling them with shimmering fairy dust. Instantly, Rachel and Kirsty shrank down to the same size as Lisa. Fluttering their wings with delight, the girls rose up into the air to join their friend.

"Follow the lollipop trail!" Lisa called, and they flew off down High Street together.

"The goblins must have *lots* of lollipops," Kirsty said with a frown, looking at the lollipop sticks and wrappers lying all over the sidewalk. "And they're eating them superfast! Look at all this garbage."

"Don't worry, Kirsty," Lisa assured her. "I can clean it up in two shakes of a fairy's wand!" As they flew along, Lisa began waving her wand over the sidewalk. Clouds of fairy magic floated down, and the lollipop litter behind them vanished!

The lollipop trail turned halfway down High Street. Lisa and the girls followed it through the winding streets of Wetherbury. Eventually, they reached the local park — and Rachel gave an excited shout.

"The trail ends here," she pointed out

as Lisa's magic whisked away the very last lollipop stick. "The goblins must be in the park!"

Kirsty, Rachel, and Lisa flew through the park gates. Up ahead, they could see four boys sitting at one of the wooden picnic tables on the grass. The boys wore matching green overalls and baseball caps, and they were all licking giant lollipops. The picnic table was covered with lots of bags from the village candy shop — all full of lollipops!

Then Rachel noticed four pairs of big

green feet sticking out from underneath the table.

"It's definitely the goblins!" she whispered with a grin.

"Let's hide close by and listen to what they're saying," Lisa suggested.

Lisa and the girls swooped down and fluttered silently into a flower bed near the picnic table. They tucked themselves between the golden daffodils and then peeked out to see what the goblins were up to.

"Mmm!" The biggest goblin sighed happily. "These lollipops are delicious!" He finished the one he was eating and tossed the stick into the flower bed. It flew toward Rachel, and she had to duck out of the way at the last minute. Then the goblin grabbed another lollipop and pulled off the wrapper. He threw the wrapper into the daffodils, and it landed on top of Lisa. Kirsty and Rachel rushed to help her shake it off.

"You're being greedy!" the smallest goblin said to the biggest one. "You've had more yummy lollipops than anyone else." He gobbled down the rest of his lollipop and immediately grabbed two more.

"Stop that!" yelled the other two goblins. "We love the lollipops, too!" They both gobbled the rest of their lollipops as fast as possible so that they could each take another one.

"The goblins are enjoying the lollipops an awful lot," Lisa murmured. "My lollipop charm is making the lollipops taste good to them, so that means it must be close by! But where?"

Rachel, Kirsty, and Lisa stayed hidden,

hoping the goblins might mention Lisa's lollipop charm—but they didn't. Instead, they ate their way steadily through the huge pile of lollipops. After a while, Rachel noticed that the goblins' faces were looking even greener than usual.

"I don't feel good," the smallest goblin moaned. "I ate too many lollipops. I feel sick!"

"I have a tummy ache," the biggest goblin groaned, holding his stomach. "But I want just *one* more lollipop. And I've saved the best for last!"

The biggest goblin put his hand into the front pocket of his overalls. As he pulled out a beautiful, rainbow-colored lollipop, Rachel and Kirsty noticed a bracelet around the goblin's wrist. It was glimmering slightly with a magical glow.

"It's my lollipop charm!" Lisa whispered, her face bright with excitement.

Gobbling Goblins!

Lisa, Rachel, and Kirsty burst out of the
cluster of daffodils and flew straight
toward the picnic table.

"That's my lollipop charm bracelet!"
Lisa called out.

The big goblin scowled as Lisa and the
girls hovered in the air in front of him.

"Go away, you pesky fairies!" the goblin shouted, shaking his fist. "Jack Frost gave me this bracelet and told me to look after it. You're not getting it back!"

"It's helping us collect *lots* of delicious lollipops for Jack Frost," the smallest goblin said proudly.

"We need them to make lollipop flowers for the garden at Jack Frost's candy castle," the big goblin added.

Kirsty pointed down at the lollipop sticks and wrappers and the empty bags strewn on the ground around the picnic table. "Exactly how many lollipops *do* you have left for Jack Frost?" Kirsty asked.

The goblins looked down at the empty picnic table.

"You ate all the lollipops, didn't you?" said Kirsty.

The goblins glanced nervously at one another. Rachel could see that they were beginning to panic.

"This is all your fault for being so greedy!" the biggest goblin told the smallest one. "Now we don't have any lollipops for Jack Frost's garden."

"*You* ate more lollipops than me!" the smallest goblin screeched. "I hardly ate any."

"What are we going to do?" asked one of the other two goblins. "We can't go back to the candy castle without any lollipops. Jack Frost will be *really* angry with us!"

"Maybe we can help you," Rachel said, raising an eyebrow.

"How?" the goblins chorused eagerly.

"If you give Lisa her lollipop charm, she'll be able to use her magic to make lots of beautiful lollipop flowers for you," Rachel told them. "Won't you, Lisa?"

Lisa nodded.

"Then Jack Frost will be *very* happy with you," Rachel added, "and you won't get into trouble."

"But first you have to clean up this mess!" Kirsty said, pointing at the garbage surrounding the picnic table. She flew down and picked up one of the lollipop wrappers.

The goblins shook their heads stubbornly.

"No way!" the biggest goblin said, hiding Lisa's lollipop charm behind his back. "Go away and leave us alone!"

"Well, OK," said Rachel. "I just wonder what Jack Frost will do when he finds out you ate all the lollipops for his garden. . . ."

The goblins all turned pale green.

"Wait!" the biggest goblin called as Rachel, Kirsty, and Lisa pretended to fly away. "Don't go!"

"So, do you agree to give Lisa her lollipop charm back *and* clean up the garbage?" Rachel asked, turning back to look at them.

Lollipop Flowers

"Yes!" the biggest goblin snapped. "Here, take it!" He held the charm bracelet out to Lisa.

Lisa swooped down and took her bracelet from the goblin. It shimmered with magic as it shrank to its Fairyland size. She fastened it on her wrist.

"Now you need to keep your end of the bargain!" the big goblin demanded. "Where are our lollipop flowers?"

Lisa waved her wand and released a burst of magic sparkles. A gorgeous red lollipop in the shape of a rose

appeared on the picnic table. The goblins howled with rage.

"One lollipop flower isn't enough for Jack Frost's garden!" the smallest goblin yelled. "You promised us lots and lots!"

"And you'll get lots more," Lisa replied, "*after* you clean up the garbage like you promised."

Grumbling loudly, the goblins began to pick up all the bags, lollipop wrappers, and sticks. Lisa's magic made Rachel and

Kirsty human-size again, and they
helped the goblins throw the trash into
the garbage cans.

When they were finished, Lisa waved
her wand again. With a flash of glittering
sparkles, four large, green wheelbarrows
appeared. Rachel and Kirsty saw that
each wheelbarrow was crammed full with
lollipops in the shape of flowers — daisies,
roses, tulips, daffodils, and even giant
lollipop sunflowers!

The goblins were thrilled. They dashed over to the wheelbarrows and examined the lollipop flowers with glee.

"These look good enough to eat!" the biggest goblin exclaimed.

"No!" groaned the other three goblins. "We feel sick!"

"You're the greediest goblin of all!" the smallest goblin told the big one. Arguing loudly, each goblin grabbed a wheelbarrow and hurried away.

Lisa, Rachel, and Kirsty grinned at one another.

"Girls, thank you so much for helping me get my magic lollipop charm back just before the big goblin took a bite!" Lisa laughed. "I couldn't have done it without you. And now I must return to the Fairyland Candy Factory and give everyone the good news. At least there will be lollipops for Treat Day!" Lisa disappeared with a wink, leaving a faint mist of fairy magic behind her.

Just then, the girls suddenly noticed two

pretty bouquets of flowers lying on the
picnic table. When they looked a little
closer, they realized that the flowers were
lollipops—lollipops that looked like pink
roses, white tulips, and yellow daisies.

Tucked inside each bouquet
was a tiny note, written
on glittery paper. The
notes read: *Thank you
for all your help! Love, Lisa.*

"Aren't these lollipop flowers pretty?"
Kirsty said happily, admiring her
bouquet as she and Rachel headed back
to High Street.

"Yes, they're far too beautiful to
eat—no matter what the goblins say!"
Rachel laughed.

As they got close to the village candy
shop, the girls could see Tracy Twist

outside, waving to some happy
customers.

"Look, it's Mom and Aunt Helen!"
Kirsty exclaimed. Hiding their fairy
bouquets behind their backs, the girls ran
to catch up with Mrs. Tate and Aunt
Helen. Rachel
and Kirsty
grinned at each
other when
they saw that
both Mrs. Tate
and Aunt Helen
were licking
brightly colored
lollipops!

"Hello, girls,"
said Aunt Helen. "We just
popped by to see Tracy Twist, who's an

old friend of mine, and she gave us these lollipops. They're delicious!"

"They certainly are," Kirsty's mom agreed.

"Maybe things are starting to get better at Candy Land," Aunt Helen murmured hopefully. "But I'm still worried. The lollipops are back to normal, but we're still having a lot of other problems at the factory."

Kirsty glanced at Rachel. She knew exactly what her friend was thinking. It was wonderful that they'd managed to find Lisa's lollipop charm.

But Jack Frost was determined to build his candy castle, and it would be up to Rachel and Kirsty to stop him. They had to find the other six Sugar and Spice Fairies' magical charms — no matter what it took!

THE SUGAR AND SPICE FAIRIES

Now it's time for
Kirsty and Rachel to help

Esme
the Ice Cream Fairy!

Read on for a special sneak peek. . . .

"Bye, Aunt Helen," said Kirsty Tate, hugging her aunt. "It was really nice to see you again."

"Thanks for all the candy," added Rachel Walker, Kirsty's best friend. She was staying with Kirsty over spring break.

Aunt Helen smiled at them. "My pleasure," she said. "I'm sorry they weren't as good as usual, though."

Kirsty's aunt had the best job in the world: She worked at Candy Land, the treat factory just outside of Wetherbury. She'd come to have lunch with the Tates that day, bringing a big bag of Candy Land goodies for everyone. Unfortunately, the candy had tasted terrible. Something had gone horribly wrong!

The girls were disappointed—but their dismay had quickly turned to excitement when their friend Honey the Candy Fairy magically appeared in Kirsty's bedroom! She told them that strange things had been happening at her Fairyland Candy Factory, and asked if they'd help her.

Kirsty and Rachel hadn't hesitated for

a second. Of course they'd help—they
loved going to Fairyland! And so they'd
been swept up in another wonderful
fairy adventure, this time with Honey
and her team of Sugar and Spice Fairies.
It had been the most perfect start to the
week, Rachel thought, smiling to herself.

The girls, Aunt Helen, and Kirsty's
mom were now standing outside Tracy
Twist's candy shop in Wetherbury,
where Aunt Helen was catching the
bus back to work. "I hope everything's
working the way it should at Candy
Land again," she said. "At least the
lollipops were good."

"The lollipops were *delicious*," Kirsty
replied, with a secret wink at Rachel.
Earlier that day, the two of them had
met Lisa the Lollipop Fairy. They had

a thrilling time tracking down her magic lollipop charm, which had been stolen by wicked Jack Frost. Lisa used her magic charm to make lollipops everywhere lickable, and while it was missing they had tasted horrible. Luckily, Kirsty and Rachel had helped Lisa get it back. Now all the lollipops were yummier than ever!

"Good," Aunt Helen said. "I left a special surprise for you back at your house, which I hope you like, too." She grinned at the girls. "Ah, here comes my bus. Good-bye, all of you. Thanks for a lovely lunch!"

"Bye!" chorused Kirsty, Rachel, and Mrs. Tate, waving to Aunt Helen as the bus drove away.

"I wonder what the surprise is," Kirsty

said, once the bus was out of sight.

"Knowing Aunt Helen, it's something really good," Mrs. Tate said with a smile.

Rachel smiled, too, and felt a fluttery feeling inside at the thought of a surprise waiting for them. Whenever she and Kirsty got together, life was always full of surprises!

They headed back toward Kirsty's house. As they walked through the market square, Rachel found herself looking out for more fairies. Honey had a team of seven Sugar and Spice Fairies, who helped her create delicious treats using their special magic charms. Unfortunately, Jack Frost had decided that he wanted all their yummy treats for himself. He was planning to build a gigantic Candy Castle! He had ordered his goblins to steal the magical charms, so he could make the best treats ever. Unfortunately, while the charms were away from their fairy owners, candy and treats didn't look or taste as good as usual!

Even worse, this had all happened just before the fairies' annual Treat Day! This was the day when Queen Titania and King Oberon gave every fairy a basket full of treats as a special thank-you for their hard work all year. It looked like those baskets would remain empty—unless the girls could help the Sugar and Spice Fairies get their magic charms back from the goblins.